The Front Hall Carpet

by Nicholas Heller

GREENWILLOW BOOKS, New York

For the Conte family

Watercolor and acrylic paints and a
black pen were used for the full-color art.
The text type is Brighton Light.

Printed in Singapore by Tien Wah Press
First Edition

10 9 8 7 6 5 4 3 2 1

Library of Congress
Cataloging-in-Publication Data
Heller, Nicholas.
The front hall carpet / Nicholas Heller.
p.   cm.
Summary: A youngster lives in a house
where a blue river flows in the front hall,
a grassy green field covers the dining room,
and a maze traps night monsters in the bedroom.
ISBN 0-688-05272-X.
ISBN 0-688-05273-8 (lib. bdg.)
[1. Rugs—Fiction.]   I. Title.
PZ7.H37426Fr   1990
[E]—dc20   89-38360   CIP   AC

Our front hall carpet is blue like a river.

Sometimes I go on canoe trips

and catch speckled trout for lunch.

And sometimes I go swimming with the crocodiles.

The dining room carpet is as green as a grassy field.

It's perfect for a game of croquet

or a picnic and a nap in the shade of a cherry tree.

The tile floor in the kitchen is like a jewel-studded palace.

A long hallway leads to the throne room

where I sit and rule my loyal subjects.

There's a white, shaggy bear in our living room.

He's my friend and lets me ride on his back through the snow.

Often we see seals, and penguins floating by on icebergs.

When it gets too cold, we stop and drink hot tea with an Eskimo.

My parents have a polka-dot rug in their bedroom.

When I'm wearing red, I can only step on the red dots.

And when I'm wearing green, I have to step on the green ones.

But when I have my polka-dot pajamas on, I can step wherever I like.

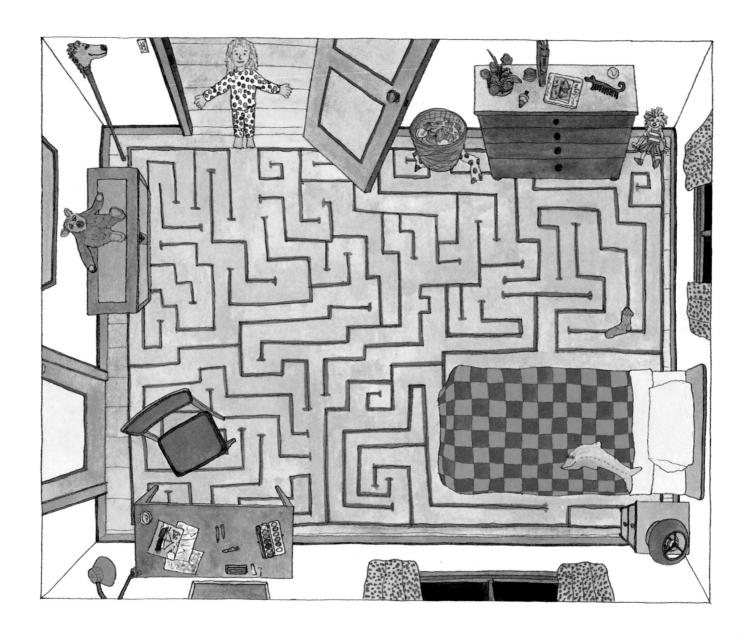

My favorite carpet is the one in my room. It's a maze.

Only I know how it works.

If any monsters try to follow me at night, they're sure to get lost.

But if you're coming to say good night,
then perhaps I'll show you the way through.

THE DUMB BUNNIES
GO TO THE ZOO

Story by Sue Denim • Pictures by Dav Pilkey

THE BLUE SKY PRESS / AN IMPRINT OF SCHOLASTIC INC.   NEW YORK

For Mary Ann, the Professor, and the rest   S. D.

For my nephews, Aaron and Connor Mancini   D. P.

THE BLUE SKY PRESS

Text copyright © 1997 by Sue Denim
Illustrations copyright © 1997 by Dav Pilkey

For information regarding permission, please write to:
Permission Department,
The Blue Sky Press, an imprint of Scholastic Inc.,
555 Broadway, New York, New York 10012.

The Blue Sky Press is a registered trademark of Scholastic Inc.

Library of Congress Cataloging-in-Publication Data
Denim, Sue, 1966-
The Dumb Bunnies go to the zoo / story by Sue Denim;
pictures by Dav Pilkey.   p.   cm.
Summary: When the Dumb Bunnies visit the zoo they
let all the animals out of their cages because they mistake
a butterfly for an escaped lion.
ISBN 0-590-84735-X
[1. Humorous stories. 2. Rabbits—Fiction. 3. Zoos—
Fiction.] I. Pilkey, Dav, 1966- ill. II. Title.
PZ7.D4149Dw 1997 [E]--dc20 96-19984 CIP AC

12 11 10 9 8 7 6 5 4 3 2 1   7 8 9/9 0/0

Printed in the United States of America
First printing, February 1997

The illustrations in this book were done with watercolors,
acrylics, India ink, low-fat vanilla yogurt, creamed asparagus,
and Tang Instant Breakfast Drink.

One morning in October, the Dumb Bunnies went outside to pick things in their garden.

Momma Bunny was picking her flowers,

Poppa Bunny was picking his vegetables . . .

. . . and Baby Bunny was picking his nose.
"That's my boy!" said Poppa Bunny.

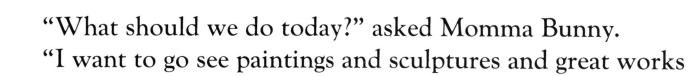

"What should we do today?" asked Momma Bunny.

"I want to go see paintings and sculptures and great works of art," said Baby Bunny.

"I know just the place," said Poppa Bunny.

So they headed off to the zoo.

When they got to the zoo, the Dumb Bunnies ran over to the ticket man.

"Duh, hi, lady," said Poppa Bunny.

"We'll take four tickets," said Momma Bunny.

"One for each of us," said Baby Bunny.

Inside the zoo, the Dumb Bunnies got
some ice cream and began to look around.

First they saw a tiny white creature standing on a sign.
"What's that animal?" asked Baby Bunny.
"Duh," said Poppa Bunny. "The sign says 'Elephant.'"
"I didn't know elephants had wings and feathers,"
said Momma Bunny.
"Me neither," said Poppa Bunny. "We sure are
learning a lot of things at the zoo."

Next they came to a cage and saw another tiny creature standing on a sign.

"What's that animal?" asked Baby Bunny.

"Duh," said Poppa Bunny. "The sign says 'Lion.'"

LION

"That can't be a lion," said Momma Bunny.
"Lions have stripes!"
"You're right," said Poppa Bunny.

Suddenly, the strange creature fluttered off the sign and landed right on Momma Bunny's arm.

"Look, Momma," cried Baby Bunny. "It does have stripes!"

"Then it must be a LION!" screamed Momma Bunny.
"HELP! HELP! THE LION HAS ESCAPED!"

All at once the zoo was in a panic.
Everyone ran off screaming, "The lion is loose!"

Poppa and Baby Bunny ran to each of the animal cages
and opened the doors.

"THE LION IS LOOSE!" they screamed. "RUN FOR YOUR LIVES!" And the animals scattered in fear.

Soon, the police arrived to capture the dangerous lion.
"Where's the lion, ma'am?" asked the police chief.

"He flew away," said Momma Bunny.

After that, the Dumb Bunnies decided
it was time to go home.
"Weeeeee!" cried Baby Bunny.

On their way back to the parking lot, they came across two more strange creatures.

"What are those big animals?" asked Baby Bunny.

"Duh," said Poppa Bunny. "The box says 'Free Kitties.'"

"I wonder how much they cost?" asked Momma Bunny.

"Can I keep them?" asked Baby Bunny.
"All right," said Momma and Poppa Bunny.
"But only if you promise not to take care of them."
"I promise," said Baby Bunny.

Poppa Bunny tied Baby Bunny's new kitties
to the roof of the car.
"Duh, they'll be safe up here," he said.

The whole way home, Baby Bunny talked and talked about his new kitties.

"I sure do love my new kitties!" said Baby Bunny.
"I'm going to name them Pee-Pee and Wee-Wee."

Seconds later, the Dumb Bunnies pulled into their garage.
"The kitties are gone," said Poppa Bunny.
"Duh, what kitties?" asked Baby Bunny.

By now, it was getting late, so the Dumb Bunnies went
inside and put on their new pajamas.
"I got these at a half-off sale!" said Momma Bunny.
"I thought so," said Poppa Bunny.

Then they crawled into their new water bed.
"This was the best week we've had all day,"
said Baby Bunny.
"That's my boy," said Poppa Bunny.

And as the sun set slowly in the East,
the Dumb Bunnies turned on all their lights,
said, "Good morning," and fell fast asleep.